'Vampire' Stories
Anna Elizabeth

Contents

'Vampire'
Stories

'Vampire' Stories

The streets of New Orleans thrummed with life, the vibrant energy of the city washing over Anna Leigh Grace as she stepped out of her cramped, small apartment. Placing her long blonde hair into a messy bun, she popped her sunglasses over her emerald, green eyes, and head for downtown. It was her first day at the Crescent Chronicle, a charming little newspaper nestled in the heart of the business district. With its weathered brick facade and vintage sign, it beckoned to dreamers and storytellers alike.

"Welcome to the Crescent Chronicles, where every story is a heartbeat away from the extraordinary!" Joseph had said with a warm smile that sent a thrill through her. He was the actual owner, editor, and lead writer, an imposing figure with tousled brown hair, striking blue eyes, and an inexplicable aura of charisma that drew her in. As Anna settled into her desk, surrounded by high stacks of yellowed pages and typewriters, she couldn't help but glance over at Joseph. He was hunched over his own desk across the room, furiously typing on his computer, coconuts wafting his wake. She was intrigued by the little details that surrounded his open office: the antique globe, the collection of the many vintage leather vampire novels that lined the bookshelf behind his desk, and a peculiar assortment of trinkets that hinted at his eccentricity. There were several ancient, old artifacts lining the walls on mahogany shelves.

As Anna was gazing just a little too hard, Joseph looked up from his typing. Quickly, Anna turned her ahead, as if she was busy arranging her own desk. Joseph chuckled as he stood and made his way across the massive room of editors who were busy writing their articles, approaching Anna's desk, he asked, "What's your first column about?" As he rested against her desk, her workstation, his gaze seeming to be so penetrating.

"Romance," she replied, a hint of a shy smile tugging her lips. "Love stories that can withstand anything, I think, will be my first article."

Joseph raised an eyebrow, curiosity piqued, "Including immortality?"

Anna felt a slight flutter of surprise at his question as she glanced up at him, "Are you suggesting a vampire romance?"

"Why not?" his mere grin widened, revealing just a hint of a fang. "After all, it is New Orleans."

Anna laughed a small laugh, as Joseph returned to his office. She was in deep thought after seeing his fang, but like he had said, this was New Orleans, and many individuals have fang implants now.

Days turned into weeks, as Anna became fully settled in her role, her job. A career that required many late-night hours, since Joseph only ran his newspaper through the nighttime shifts. Her column was seemingly going well, yet she found herself increasingly captivated by Joseph. Their passing conversations flowed effortlessly, weaving through topics of literature, the city's rich history, and the art of mesmerizing storytelling. The more time she spent with him, the more she felt drawn to the enigma he embodied, yet there was something very peculiar about Joseph. He never seemed to eat lunch, or anything; instead, he would casually mention his 'diet', which involved visiting hospitals and purchasing blood bags. At first, Anna thought he was just really obsessed with the mere belief that he was immortal, a vampire. She brushed it off as a quirky detail... until the night she actually caught a mere glimpse of his reflection in the clear, office window, or rather, the lack thereof.

"Joseph, do you..." she began, her heart pounding in her chest, nervously.

"You're wondering if I am a 'real' vampire?" he interrupted, his voice low and calm. "You are clever, Anna Leigh Grace. I admire that."

Instead of recoiling in fear, Anna found herself slightly fascinated at the idea that Joseph might actually be a 'real' vampire, "So, you are real, a real, actual vampire?"

"Very much so," he replied, confident, a shadow of slight pride, yet a hint of sadness flickering across his pale features. "And you don't fear me?"

"Not yet," Anna teased, her heart fluttering.

Joseph went straight to his office and began working on his computer, while Anna pondered on his question, 'should I fear him?' Anna's heart continued to race inside her chest, Joseph seemed so open about being immortal. If he was a real vampire, he did not try to hide it. Yet, it seemed no one in the office actually really believed him.

As autumn descended upon the city, Anna's relationship with Joseph seemed to deepen. She often caught him staring at her from his office. Late-night discussions morphed into several lingering gazes and secret stolen moments. Anna's heart torn between fascination and slight fear. She learned of Joseph's struggles, how he actually fought against the primal urge to bite her and consume her blood, the mere taste of her blood was so tempting, while simultaneously wanting to hold her close to him. Anna always blushed at these comments, yet she feared them too.

One balmy, late evening, as her and Joseph was the only ones remaining in the newspaper, they found themselves wandering through the French Quarter, after much conversation on an article about 'vampires' roaming in the Quarter, they had agreed to stroll the many streets in search of any evidence to write about. The moon casting a bright glow on the cobblestone streets, "You know," Joseph began, his voice barely above a whisper, "I have spent many centuries here, alone. The thought of being with someone... it actually terrifies me."

Anna turned to him, spitting her coffee from her lips, nervously, her expression softening, blushing, "Well, you don't have to be alone anymore, Joseph. I don't want to run away from you, immortal or not, I'm right here to stay."

"I want to keep you close to me, Anna. I have felt some strong feelings for you, for some time now. I want to keep you safe, especially from me." he confessed, his blue eyes filled with slight pain that was becoming evident.

"But I am not really afraid of you, Joseph," she murmured, stepping closer to him, "I think I have started falling for you."

In the few weeks that followed, Anna and Joseph navigated the delicate balance of their new relationship. Each night was a dance between passion and restraint. Joseph gifted her with his undead heart, a mere treasure that she guarded fiercely, and Anna kept his true secret close, the actual knowledge of his immortality that was 'real', while others still believed him to be insane, obsessed with the supernatural. This true knowledge was a secret bond between them that drew them all the more closer to each other. Joseph even trusted Anna enough to actually drink blood in front of her, the blood from the blood bags, that he kept in his office, hidden in the small refrigerator under his massive desk.

Anna began incorporating their unique love story, their mere fantasy, into her romance column, weaving the threads of their unconventional, estranged connection into her writing. The city buzzed with many tales of vampires and love, and Anna found herself immortalized in the very ink she cherished, in the very stories she wrote.

One night, while they strolled together through the moonlit park, Joseph paused, gazing at Anna with an intensity that made her heart skip a beat inside her chest. "You've changed everything for me, Anna Leigh Grace," he whispered in her ear as his cool lips brushed her earlobe. "You have struck my undead heart with a forming love that could conquer even the darkest of fears."

Anna blushed, becoming really warm inside herself, as Joseph spoke her full name. "Then let's face our fears together, Joseph." she replied, her voice steady, yet nervous. "No secrets. We will always be honest with one another."

Several months passed, and the Crescent Chronicles flourished under their joint stewardship. Anna's romance column became a beloved feature throughout the city of New Orleans, and the mere love story of their personal relationship captivated the many readers. She wrote of their estranged relationship of a mere mortal woman falling in love with a vampire, a creature of the night. Joseph learned to intertwine his immortality with the world of the living, of today's culture and style, with Anna by his side. Their laughter, their romance echoing through the busy streets of the city of New Orleans.

Though the city thrived, the shadows never really left him, but with Anna, he found solace in the mere light she radiated. She was his sunlight, and he would forever remain her vampire, a mere love that seemed to transcend time itself, immortal in every sense of the word. In the heart of New Orleans, amidst the many stories they would create, Joseph knew that he had finally found his true companion, that he had found his place, not just in the world, but in Anna's beating heart. Joseph knew that their time together would seem fleeting in his eyes, he knew that one day, Anna would have to leave him, she would have to leave this world, but he was determined to love her until that day would come. Thoughts of actually changing her, giving her this mere immortality played heavily through his mind on many occasions, but he just could not bring himself to actually harm her, or curse her with this torment.

Joseph stayed positive, only focusing on the mere idea that Anna's mortal life was a spark, intense and beautiful. He would savor every moment, every laugh, every kiss, always savoring even the bittersweet moments, the mere nature of their estranged love.

Anna and Joseph slowly, over time, created a world together. They married after several years and settled into the outskirts of the city in a two-story Victorian home. They were happy, yet Anna's health was faltering. Anna had become elder and very fragile, while Joseph remained the same. He loved her more and more each passing day that they were together. Joseph sold the newspaper some years ago, after he and Anna traveled the world, seeing many places and many amazing sights. They even bought many t-shirts to prove where they had visited.

One dim evening, as the heavy clouds illuminated the sky of New Orleans, Joseph and Anna found themselves on their top floor balcony. Anna was comfortably resting under a wool blanket as Joseph cuddled next to her fragile, aging body. The air was cool, yet pleasing, filled with the scent of magnolias that exceeded their backyard, and the faint sound of jazz music echoed from the window where a small radio was resting.

"Do you remember our very first night in the French Quarter together, Joseph?" Anna vaguely spoke, her voice faint, weakened.

"The first night you finally admitted to me that you were falling for me?"

"Of course, I will always remember that night," Joseph replied, his voice soft as he turned his gaze to hers, "You captivated my very being that night, especially after the passionate kiss that you had surprised me with."

Anna laughed a struggling laugh, a small chuckle of love, that sent a secret thrill through Joseph as he smiled, his fangs showing vividly.

"And you still haven't ever bitten me." Anna stated, as she smiled a fragile smile at him.

Joseph leaned closer, his undead heart pounding in his chest, "I have always wanted to, Anna, I always will, but you taught to value your mortal life, to see the beauty in living, to feel the sorrow in a life passing to the great beyond. I have learned from you, to always see the miraculous beauty in living a mortal existence."

Their eyes locked, and in that moment, the entire world around them seemed to fade away. All Joseph could see was Anna, with her warm, radiant beauty, even though the aging process had faltered her appearance, she was still so beautiful.

"Promise me something, Joseph," she said, her voice barely above a whisper, "Promise me that you will always carry our story with you, no matter where your immortal life takes you. That you will remember me, always, even when the many years stretch into your eternity."

He reached for her fragile hand, intertwining their fingers, "I promise, Anna. I will never forget you. You will always be my greatest adventure. I will carry your memory with me forever, deep within my undead heart."

With a gentle pull, Joseph brought her closer to him in his arms, their foreheads touching, the night sky filled with promising rain clouds, and that sacred moment, time seemed to stand still... Anna was gone.

Joseph wept many blood tears as he slowly brushed a stand of blonde hair behind her ear, just gazing at the beauty, the love, he will never forget.

Joseph left that lovely Victorian home, returning to the French Quarter. As he walked the dirty, darkened streets alone, under the watchful gaze of the full moon, he embraced the sorrow, the joyful memories of his only true love, Anna Leigh Grace. He embraced the fleeting time he had shared with her, the love they had known, like the ink in a cherished story; it would live on forever even after the last page was turned. As a small blood tear rolled down his cheek, Joseph pondered on the mere memory of when him and Anna had first stepped into their home, their Victorian house... he remembered how their story was not one that just happened overnight, it was the kind of sweet love that matured over the years, ripening like fine wine that only got better with age. They had met in the simple, yet busy newspaper, the Crescent Chronicles, brought together by their mere passion of writing. His kind yet mystifying blue eyes had captivated Anna from the start, yet it took patience and simple tenderness to completely win her over. Anna was so graceful and full of life; she was the perfect complement to his steady and unwavering nature. Together, they created a world of their own... a mere life built on love, trust, and small, shared dreams. They had traveled to far-off places, collecting many artifacts, souvenirs, and several unforgettable memories that Joseph would always cherish for eternity. Each small relic they collected during their tour of the world would be a testament to the places they had been, where they had shared many intimate, romantic moments together.

Joseph remembered all the different cultures they had explored while on their travels, and the adventures they had embarked side by side. Yet, no matter where their travels took them, they always found their way back to their true sanctuary, a place Joseph will always remember, always remember the many memories they created there... a home they made together, a place they had chosen and lovingly nurtured over the years. All the relics and memories still remained in this abandoned Victorian home. It was not just a mere house; it was a symbol of their journey together. It was a place where their laughter echoed through the hallways, where quiet moments of comfort was shared on many occasions, and where their love story had continued to unfold, night after night. The old house was more than wood and stone; it was a mere witness to their undying love, a small testament of their shared history, and a refuge where they would face the challenges of life, of time together.

Joseph remembered how Anna and himself had chosen to live on the outskirts of the city, away from any busy crowds of people, away from any hustle and bustle, in a place where they could enjoy the serenity of nature. Their two-story home was like a masterpiece, tucked away from the city streets of New Orleans, resting gracefully at the end of a tree-lined avenue, as many magnolia trees stood proudly. The mere journey to their massive home was a simple winding path, with a canopy of oak and maple trees mixed with many magnolia trees, a few cypress trees stood in the distance accenting the beautiful aroma of the property. These trees provided shade, privacy, creating an almost enchanted feel as if one was walking into a magical, different time. The house itself stood proudly, showing its age vaguely, amidst a sprawling flower garden. It was painted a soft shade of ivory, with accents of sage green on the many shutters and trim that framed its tall, elegant windows. The front porch was long and inviting, wrapping around the side of the grand house, adorned with wicker chairs and a swing that creaked ever so gently in the breeze. The massive porch was a place where he and Anna spent so many evenings, just watching the stars twinkle in the sky, as they cuddled on the relaxing sway of the wooden swing.

As you approached this beauty of the house, the first thing that captured your eye was the intricate detailing on the gables, with carved wooden trims that told stories of much craftsmanship from a bygone era. The Victorian-style architecture gave the house an air of time-lessness, as if it had stood there for many centuries, witnessing the changing seasons and the ebb and flow of many lives. The large bay windows, which were a major hallmark of Victorian design, allowed the moonlight to flood into the rooms, filling the house with warmth and dim light. The front door, a sturdy oak piece with a brass knocker shaped like a lion's head, was a grand entrance into the mere world that Anna and Joseph had blissfully created together. The heavy door itself was a deep, rich mahogany, polished to perfection, with an ornate glass panel etched with a hint of faded, floral patterns. This door had witnessed many, countless moments, a symbol of both arrivals and departures, of many new beginnings and farewells.

Joseph remembered when they had first stepped inside of the beautiful home, you were greeted by a foyer that whispered of old-world charm and elegance. The floor was a mosaic black and white tiles, leading into the heart of the house. The walls became lined with many portraits of Anna, many photographs of nature and flowers, just a mere visual timeline of Joseph's life with her, though his picture was not there, his immortality would not allow such a caption. Many photographs in frames hung along the walls that held many memories of their travels together. An ornate chandelier hung from the ceiling, its crystal droplets catching the light and casting a soft glow around the room. Beneath it was a small table adorned with a vase of fresh flowers, an arrangement that he changed regularly every late evening, always selecting Anna's favorites. This was the essence of their home; it was full of their estranged love, their estranged life, relationship, their marriage, and small gestures that spoke of a deep, unspoken bond between them.

The living room was a cozy, inviting space, filled with an electric mix of furniture that spoke to the couple's estranged travels and a variety of their tastes. It was a room that told unspoken stories, every piece of furniture had its place, its history. There was an old, leather Chesterfield sofa in a deep, worn brown that sat against one wall, accompanied by a pair of overstuffed armchairs, each draped with a handmade quilt. The soft quilts were creations of Anna's grandmother, she had them ever since she was a small child. The fireplace was the focal point of the massive room, a grand structure made of stone, with a wooden mantle that held an assortment of framed photos, candles, and small trinkets from their travels. Above the mantle was a large, antique clock, its pendulum swinging rhythmically, a reminder of time's relentless march forward, yet also a symbol of the precious moments shared within these old walls. On the coffee table lay an assortment of Joseph's vintage vampire books, books of literature that were evident in the diverse collection that spanned everything from classic novels to travel journals. Beside the books were several antique newspapers from past days at the Crescent Chronicles, years of worn pages from being flipped through and browsed through. This living room was where Joseph and Anna would spend their evenings most nights. Anna curled up in a blanket with a book, while Joseph read quietly to himself next to her on the couch.

The kitchen was Anna's most pleasing domain, a place that brought her immense joy. It was a spacious sunlit room, that Joseph seldom avoided. It had large windows that looked out onto the flower garden. The cabinetry was a soft, pastel blue, complementing the cream-colored walls. The countertops were made of polished oak, their surfaces gleaming with a well-maintained shine. The kitchen island in the center was where Anna would prepare herself small meals, while preparing larger meals for the community center in the city. Anna loved to donate the food she had made to the hungry, while I slept throughout the day hours. Her hands deftly moving through the motions of chopping, mixing, and stirring whatever she felt like making at that particular moment. Hanging from the ceiling were copper pots and pans, reflecting the sunlight that streamed through the massive windows during the day. The shelves were lined with many jars of herbal spices, homemade jams, and preserves, a small testament to Anna's love for cooking. She actually loved cooking more than she did her writings. The kitchen was always filled with sweet aromas, the scent of something that seemed to be delicious, though Joseph, when he'd awaken after sunset, could never get to enjoy the taste of such things, he only could sense the smell. Aromas of fresh bread baking in the oven or the rich fragrance of a stew simmering on the stove. There was a small breakfast nook by the window, where they would often sit together at night, Anna would eat her dinners there while Joseph sipped on his blood bags across from her. They shared many conversations at that small table, as they watched the faint squirrels run across the darkened grass outside. This area of the kitchen was a place of comfort, a place where time seemed to slow down for Joseph, allowing him and Anna to savor each other's company.

Connected to the kitchen was the huge dining room, a space that was mostly for mere looks. This space, this room held many expensive dishes, made of porcelain, many China plates on display that held un-forgotten memories of their travels, ones Joseph will always cherish. In the center of the room was a large oak dining table, polished to a gleam, surrounded by high-backed chairs with plush cushions. The table was often adorned with a lace tablecloth and a vintage candelabra, which Joseph would light during special occasions so that Anna could see the glow of the many candles burning. The walls were painted with a rich shade of burgundy, which was Anna's favorite color, giving the room a warm, inviting feel. The windows were draped with heavy curtains that could be drawn back during the day, letting Anna get the much-needed sunlight she deserved, before I awoke at dark. Along one wall stood a glass-fronted cabinet, filled with all the fine China, crystal glasses, and vintage silverware that had been collected over the years of their travels together. The dining room was where they stored their finer artifacts, fragile trinkets of porcelain.

Joseph remembered the massive staircase, which had always been his favorite part of the house. It led to the upper floors, as a grand, sweeping structure made of dark oak, its banister polished to a rich sheen. The steps creaked gently as you ascended, each one a note in the melody of the house. Along the walls that lined the staircase were more paintings, mere memories of Joseph and Anna together in various parts of the world, where unknown artists would paint their portraits for them. At the top of the stairs was a small landing, where a huge grandfather clock stood tall and proud, its ticking a familiar sound in the quiet of the night. The hallway branched off into several bedrooms, each with its own story to tell, each room filled with extravagant items that they had collected over the years. The master bedroom was a mere sanctuary, a private place where Anna and Joseph could retreat from the world. Joseph had his own closet, dark and set apart from the rest of the room, where his eternal slumber would take place during each day. No, it was not a coffin, but a twin bed hidden between thick walls, where no sunlight could ever enter. The master bedroom was dominated by a large, four-poster bed, its frame made of dark mahogany, with a canopy of soft, flowing fabric. The bed was covered in layers of quilts and fluffy pillows, creating a cocoon of comfort and warmth for Anna. Joseph would spend many nights on this bed with Anna, just holding her in his cool arms, watching her sleep, peacefully, after their intimate relations. The walls were painted a soft burgundy, a color Anna had chosen for its soothing effect. The large bay window let in the morning light for Anna as she would awake every morning, its thick, wool curtains could be drawn back to reveal a view of the magnolias in all their glory below. In the center of the floor was a vanity table cluttered with all of Anna's perfumes and various jewelry. There was a rocking chair in the corner where she would sit and imagine on some nights what it would be like to have a child, and how it would feel to rock that child to sleep. By the window was a small writing desk, where Anna and Joseph shared many stories together and many writings. This master bedroom was a vivid memory for him, since almost all their most romantic, intimate moments occurred there. Joseph cherished those memories, as he shed another blood tear down his cheek.

The flower garden was Anna's pride and joy during her alone time, the daylight hours, a space where she could lose herself in the simple pleasure of tending her colorful plants. This garden was a riot of colors, with beds of roses, tulips, and daffodils creating a patchwork of many hues. There was a small vegetable patch where she grew tomatoes, cucumbers, and herbs, all of which she found helpful with her cooking. A cobblestone path wound its way through the flower garden, leading to a small gazebo draped in ivy, where Joseph and Anna would sit most nights and enjoy the cool evening breeze under the stars as they twinkled high above in the sky. The garden was a place of reflection for them, of peace, and it was where Joseph often found himself after Anna would retire to bed. Sitting alone for a while, before the sun decided to rise, he would get lost in his thoughts.

Joseph remembered the years slowly, he remembered when Anna's health started to decline, how she became so frail; her once vibrant spirit dimming, but his love for her only deepened. She was his constant companion, his protector through the daylight hours, his true, loyal friend, his only love. Joseph tried his very best to care for her with much devotion and mere kindness, never swaying from his devotion to her. The Victorian house had been the one witness to their love story, yet now it was merely abandoned, a quiet place of never forgotten memories, of whispered conversations, and an estranged love that had stood the test of time.

ThoughJoseph had sold his newspaper many years ago, dedicating all his time to Anna, their travels had come to an end, but he would always cherish every moment they shared. The old house simply stood as a mere testament of the life they had built together, a life filled with true love, much adventure, and an unbreakable bond of the heart, or in Joseph's case, his undead heart.

In truth, Joseph and Anna had found much solace in each other over the many years they were together. An everlasting romance that would resonate through the ages, intertwined like the roots of the ancient cypress trees that lined the entire city of New Orleans, even to the swamps that were hidden deep in the bayous. They had written their own tale, one that would for all eternity whisper in the shadows and sing in the many hearts of those who had ever dared to love.

Anna would forever be his 'Vampire' story...

The End.

'Vampire' Stories
By: Anna Elizabeth